... because of a wolf.

'Why don't you come out to play,
little creature?' asks the wolf.

'I'm sure we'd be **VERY** good friends.'

'No, thank you,' replies the little creature.
'I already have two friends.'

So the little creature stays home.

The wolf comes back day after day.

'Why don't you come out to play,
little creature?' asks the wolf.
'I bet you're SO bored in there,
all cooped up in your cave.'

'No, thank you,' replies the little creature.
'Only boring creatures get bored.'

So the little creature stays home.

The wolf never leaves.

Not even to go to sleep.

But the little creature never comes out.

It doesn't want to climb a tree...

or play ball...

or pick flowers...

and it definitely doesn't want to feed the birds.

'Why don't you come out to play,
little creature?' asks the wolf eventually.

'I'M GETTING HUNGRY NOW!'

'I mean... er... YOU must be
getting hungry n—"

'Aaarrrggghhbzzzzzurgh!'

The little creature sniffs.
'Now you mention it,
I am a *little* hungry.'

'Well,' says the wolf.
'I have the most tasty doughnut
here with YOUR name on it!
Why don't you come and get it?!'

'Does it have sprinkles?'
the little creature asks.

'YES!'
shouts the wolf.

And with a stretch and
a shuffle, the little creature...

COMES OUT
TO PLAY!

'I DO love doughnuts,'
says the bear.

'But I'm still a little hungry…'

'Why don't you come out
to play, little creature?'
asks the bear.

'I'm sure we'd be VERY good friends.'

for little creatures everywhere - R.H.

Brimming with creative inspiration, how-to projects, and useful information to enrich your everyday life, Quarto Knows is a favourite destination for those pursuing their interests and passions. Visit our site and dig deeper with our books into your area of interest: Quarto Creates, Quarto Cooks, Quarto Homes, Quarto Lives, Quarto Drives, Quarto Explores, Quarto Gifts, or Quarto Kids.

Inspiring | Educating | Creating | Entertaining

First published in 2017 by Lincoln Children's Books
First paperback edition published in 2018 by Lincoln Children's Books,
an imprint of The Quarto Group.
The Old Brewery, 6 Blundell Street, London N7 9BH, United Kingdom.
T (0)20 7700 6700 F (0)20 7700 8066 **www.QuartoKnows.com**

A catalogue record for this book is available from the British Library.

ISBN 978-1-78603-116-7

The illustrations were created using mixed and digital media
Set in Baskerville

Published by Rachel Williams
Designed by Andrew Watson
Edited by Katie Cotton
Production by Laura Grandi

Manufactured in Guangdong, China CC 122017

9 8 7 6 5 4 3 2 1